Anonymous

Fabellae Mostellariae

Devonshire and Wiltshire stories in verse, including specimens of the

Devonshire dialect

Anonymous

Fabellae Mostellariae
Devonshire and Wiltshire stories in verse, including specimens of the Devonshire dialect

ISBN/EAN: 9783337367596

Printed in Europe, USA, Canada, Australia, Japan

Cover: Foto ©Andreas Hilbeck / pixelio.de

More available books at **www.hansebooks.com**

A TALE OF TWO GHOSTS.

' V'là deux ! '
The Black Mousquetaire.

'Tis pleasant to view from the lofty cliffs
The spacious blue, and the fisher-skiffs;
Or watch the nibbling flocks that roam
    O'er the verdant meads, where the voices haunt
Of the incessant waves that foam
    On the beach below, with their idle vaunt.
On these fair meads, as people say,
A spectral lady, at early day,
Was wont, in years long pass'd away,
Garb'd in satin of emerald hue,
To glide o'er the grass empearl'd with dew;
No sooner seen by the startled eye,
Than lost in the air's dim vacancy.

Why did the spirit these pastures haunt?—
The tale hath a spice of old Romaunt.

B

Report was rife from an oldish date
  That *something* oftentimes was seen,
  Of gruesome and forbidding mien,
Sitting upon a certain gate
Within the bounds of Berry Farm:
But none who saw it came to harm;
Because, like reasonable creatures,
When they had glimpsed the ghastly features,
They hurried on, with fear possess'd,
And not a word to it address'd;
Excepting one, who sadly rued
That he the spirit interview'd,
And spoke to it. It is not known
  What he said, or the ghost replied;
This fact is handed down alone,
  That ere the week was out, he died.

'Tis proved it sat not there for nought;
For once when sheaves were homeward brought
At harvest-time, and with its freight
Between the posts of that same gate
A wain was passing, from the ground
Issued a dull and crashing sound:
A wheel sank down, and instantly
Stuck fast within a cavity.   ,
A trough of stone was then perceived,
Which from the earth they soon upheaved;—
A coffin!—for therein enclosed
A fleshless skeleton reposed:

The doctor said, 'A woman's frame';
But none could tell how there it came.
I had this tale from the sacristan,
John Potts, a quaint gray-headed man,
Who saw the bones, when thus reveal'd,
Where they had lain so long conceal'd.

Well! but who was she?—I will try
To give the querist a reply.
'Tis said that Farmer Bray one night
Was suddenly put in a fright:
At his bed's foot a lady stood,
So pale,—the sight quite chill'd his blood.
And, as 'twas said, the apparition
Seem'd in a very *whisht*[1] condition,
As if some weight upon her mind
Made her appear to humankind,
About which she would fain be ask'd;
But though his brains the farmer task'd,
It seems, he could find nought to say,
But silent and dumb-founder'd lay.
But when a second time the sprite
He had beheld at dead of night,
And still at the weird presence quail'd,
And to interrogate it fail'd,
He thought it proper to announce all
The circumstances to one Bounsall,

[1] sad.

The parson of the place where he
Had lived before he came to B——;
Judging it unsafe to apply
To parson S——, who lived too nigh:
So might the secret well be kept,
While old Dame Gossip soundly slept.

Thinking that he could not do better,
The farmer wrote the following letter:—
'Berry Farm, B——combe. Reverend Sir,
Don't let this put you in a stir:
I write you these few lines by post,
To say that I have seen a ghost,—
A lady's ghost,—but from my lack, sir,
Of learning, don't know what to ax her.
Please send advice without delay
To yours obediently, James Bray!'

Within a day or two there came
The parson's answer to the same.
'Dear James, of most unusual sort
Is the event which you report.
I hardly know what to suggest:
However, I have done my best,
And send a proper adjuration,
Which you can use the next occasion
When you behold the apparition,
Which, if a ghost of good condition,

Will probably some news impart.
Mind, you get well your speech by heart;
And be sure clearly to pronounce all
The words. Yours truly, T. P. Bounsall.'

A third time yet the ghost appear'd;
And Farmer Bray, though much afear'd,
Contrived to say the adjuring words,
Which sever'd, like a knife, the cords,
Of reticence, and brought to light
The secret tidings of the sprite.

'James Bray,' the spirit said, 'behold!
I, who was once of mortal mould,
Now from mortality divorced,
By law celestial am forced
The hidden reason to disclose
Which still prevents my soul's repose.
Know that, in time of civil strife,
I was a loyal soldier's wife.
My gallant husband, who embraced
His sovereign's cause, and bravely faced
The dangers of the war, nor swerved
From duty to the king he served,
Anxious to shelter me from harm,
Convey'd me to this distant farm;
And, when he left, a treasure large
Of gold committed to my charge.

He fell in fight, and while I still
Abode here, fearing nothing ill,
Some demon put it in the mind
Of the vile tenant that he'd find
Within his grasp an ample store
Of golden coin were I no more.
He smother'd me,—the miscreant base!—
With pillows press'd upon my face :
Then in a long stone trough, the tank
From which his thirsty cattle drank,
Buried me underneath a gate
   Which on the other side the road,
Between two fields of this estate,
   A bowshot is from this abode.
The trough he cover'd with a slab,
That Earth might not the secret blab.
He seized my wealth,—a large amount,—
And for my absence to account
Devised the lying tale that I,
On urgent summons, hastily
Had left the farm and gone away,
But whither gone he could not say.
He dug a hole beneath the stair,
And hid the store of money there :
But ere to any one beside
'Twas known, by sudden fit he died,
Plagued by his conscience-stricken mind,
And Providence which rules mankind.
Meanwhile, until my bones are found,
Lifted, and laid in hallow'd ground,

I haunt at morn and eventide
The pastures by the sea-cliffs' side,
Wearing the semblance of a dress
I wore when life was happiness.
Also, it is the murderer's fate,
Above my grave, upon the gate
Till then to sit, a blasting sprite,
Whether 'tis seen by day or night,
Blighting with woes and ills abhorr'd
All who address to him a word:
Those only can escape from scath
Who silent pass that direful wraith.
Further, until that treasure laid
Within the pit the murderer made,
Again shall be reveal'd to light,
I haunt this house at dead of night.
Fail not my relics to exhume,
And in the church-yard them entomb.
The treasure to the State reveal,
Which well will recompense your zeal:
This do, or you will fare the worse,
And bring upon yourself a curse.'
No more than this the spirit spake;
And left James Bray all in a quake.

Although with hopes of wealth elate,
Bray prudently resolved to wait
Till all his household forth were gone
     To some club-feast, or neighbouring fair;

Then dug, and found beneath a stone
  The treasure hid behind the stair :
The which, through sordid greed of pelf,
He kept entirely to himself,
Saying the sprite's advice was ' stuff,'
And that the farmers paid enough
Dues, they were charged with, to the State,
Under the head of tax and rate :
And with this money at command
Discharged his debts, and bought some land,
Revealing but to one or two
How he became so ' well to do.'
Also the ingrate took no pains
To disinter the sprite's remains.
Whether for this he fared the worse,
And brought upon himself the curse,
For which profanely he declared
That not a single pin he cared,
Is not quite clear. From this world's stage
He pass'd, while yet of middle age :
And certain of his friends and kin
Reported him as over-fond of gin.

The treasure found, the lady's sprite
No more was seen, at dead of night,
In Berry farm-house ; but still sate
The phantom-murderer on the gate,
Until, as 'twas decreed, the wain,
Fraught with its load of ripen'd grain,

Avail'd to break the coffin lid
Which that fair lady's relics hid:
When the aforesaid sacristan,
John Potts, that quaint gray-headed man,
Who still contrived, though palsy-stricken,
With cider draughts his blood to quicken,
Removed the bones thus strangely found,
And laid them in the church-yard's ground.

From this same sacristan you mote
Hear many a tale and anecdote.
I've heard him say that once he saw some fairies,
As Wordsworth says, 'pursuing their vagaries';
And that the most amusing pranks were play'd
By those small wights, in jackets red array'd.
Beneath a hedge they frolic'd gamesomely;
At least, so seem'd it to the old man's eye.
Perchance to the informant's failing sight
Some things appear'd not quite exactly right;
And so red leaves, beneath the breeze which dance,
Might have sufficed to furnish his romance.
Such old men often curious facts relate:
But, still, you need not credit all they state.

MORAL.

In conforming to custom I must be exact,
And a moral contrive from this tale to extract:

As a bee from a flowret-cup honey educes,
Or divine from his text draws instruction and uses.
Don't keep too much cash in your house : it is best
In a bank to locate it, or else to invest.
Don't covet another man's goods, lest, some time,
Such longing should tempt you to perpetrate crime.
If you lodgings require, when you go by the sea,
Be discreet in your choice lest you *victimised* be.
Pay all dues to the State, if a blessing you'd win :
Don't scorn good advice ; and don't take too much gin.

THE HOLE IN THE WALL.

GENTLE reader, I ask, did it ever befall
You a story to hear of a hole in a wall?
One might say 'twas a subject of little import,
Except 'twere a hole of a very rare sort:
And such was the case in the tale I repeat,
Or my muse had not ventured the subject to treat.

In a village of Devon an old house may be seen,
Where a farmer resides: the main road runs between
Its garden in front, and the churchyard close by;
Church Living 'tis hight, tho' I can't tell you why.
'Tis built on the side of a hill rather steep,
And the road makes a cutting you'd call pretty deep
At the side of the garden, the whole of whose length
Is faced by a wall of great age and some strength;
In which wall was the aperture, passage, or hole,
Which is in my tale a great part of the whole.

This entrance in height and in width did suffice
To admit *genus homo* of average size;
But so rugged, and dreary, and dark it appear'd,
That to try the experiment all were afeard.
Beside, there was partial dilapidation
Of the rude mason-work of its ancient formation,
Which made it unsafe for whoe'er might essay
To thread the recess of that dark narrow way:
And no human soul, within memory of man,
Had ever been known its deep secret to scan:
Yet 'twas ever agreed by the wisest of head,
That *somewhere*, for certain, that strange passage led;
Tho' no one at all knew how far it extended,
Nor how it develop'd, nor in what it ended.

As to why it was made, what the date of construction,
There were many suggestions, and various deduction.
The farm-house so old had perhaps been the home
Of an order religious, when all bow'd to Rome.
From its name of Church Living one might have suspected
That somehow, for sure, with the Church 'twas connected.
Here and there on the walls are seen arms, long agone
Or moulded in plaster or sculptured in stone,
Of those who, perchance, of a new faith professors,
Of this tenement old were the later possessors.
'Tis a double-built house,—a style once thought the best,—
One part north and south, and one part east and west.
Modern structures of brick, which they run up so quick,
Have nought to compare with its walls three feet thick.

But these facts or surmises are nothing at all
To account for the curious hole in the wall,
That is now seal'd with mortar and stones for a reason
Which this story intends to relate in due season.

It chanced that, one eve, at the snug Fountain Head,
A number of rustics were met, so 'tis said,
To find in their cups and discourse recreation
Agreeable after the day's occupation;
And while they enjoy'd what a bard calls 'the bowl,'
They somehow got talking about this strange hole.
Much question ensued as to what was its use:
Some said they should like, if the stones were less loose,
To try where it led; so they certainly should;
But still 'I dare not,' they let wait on 'I would,'
Like the poor cat i' th' adage. At last, one Will Abbott,
Best known for his skill in entrapping a rabbit,
Exclaim'd, 'I don't mind going into that hole,
And I a'n't a bit fear'd but I'll come out quite whole.'
'Bet five shillings you don't?'—'Bet five shillings I do!'
'Done!'—'Done!'—The excitement at something so new
Was remarkable quite. They repair'd one and all
To the scene of the curious hole in the wall.
But before the essay, some suggested a doubt
That Will Abbott would fairly explore it throughout:
So they said, 'Mind you this, if you go, we depend
You'll bring something to show that you've been to the end.'
'Ay, my boys,' answered Will; and then taking the handle
Of a candlestick furnished with lighted candle;

And having look'd round with a resolute grin,
As expressing '*Messieurs, au revoir*,' he went in!

Now leaving the rustics outside standing round,
We'll proceed with our friend on his way under ground.
And should he be thought to require an apologist,
I here may observe that a learn'd archaeologist
Will oft, in pursuit of his favourite science,
Set trouble, and risk, and expense at defiance;
And if such be the case, is it right to complain
Of the same 'noble rage' in the breast of a swain?

By the light of the candle he cautiously stept;
Indeed I might say that he, here and there, crept,
In that ruinous passage so dreary and strait,
Taking heed to his way, and regarding his pate.
A few yards—he escaped any serious contusion—
Brought the venturous wight to his journey's conclusion.
At the end of the passage, he had but to clamber
Up a stone step or two, to get into a chamber,—
A parlour, according to his own narration;
A strange *parlour* indeed, where was no *conversation*!
All stony, and gloomy, and still, as could be,
In which, by his light, nothing else could he see
But some helmets of steel! steel not rusty, but burnish'd!
With such strange things alone this apartment was furnish'd;
Very useful, no doubt, both in sieges and battles,
But queer household goods, or, as lawyers say, *chattels*.
But this was not all the explorer descried;
For a low deep recess, in the opposite side

Of the chamber, appear'd like a doorway which led
To some other apartments as gloomy and dread.
But it seem'd to the wight that to go any further,
From what he beheld, would be much like self-murther;
So, into this ante-room having made entry,
He was not inclined to inquire for the gentry
Who own'd these steel helmets. Perhaps in their hall
They had left their steel caps,—'twas a thought to appal!—
And in dining- or drawing-room were to be found;
A terrible company, one might be bound!
This having consider'd, and look'd round a bit,
He chose a steel helm, which appear'd best to fit,
Remembering his comrades' injunction express
That he should something bring as a proof of success;
And having this trophy set firm on his head,
Went on his way back from that ante-room dread.
He afterwards said he felt not quite at ease,
As he worm'd himself out through the hole by degrees;
And thought he heard murmurs which made him afraid
Lest a cold hand should on him be suddenly laid,
And straight drag him back to the vault he had left,
Where a grim grisly sprite should indict him of theft.

The rustics, expecting our hero's return,
As soon as the glimmering light they discern,
To the entrance all eagerly crowd to behold
The proof and result of this enterprise bold.
A figure appears;—but it can't be Will Abbott
Coming out of the hole like a badger or rabbit!

'Tis more like the ghost (not a little alarmer!)—
Except less completely envelop'd in armour—
Of Hamlet's good father, the glimpse of the moon
Revisiting.—Well! he came back pretty soon
In this guise which created a general start,
And paled even the cheek of the stoutest of heart;
   For it needs must occasion some wonder or dread,
To see one, in vulgar discourse term'd a 'feller,'
Coming out of a place very much like a cellar,
   With a *casque* on his head!!!

.

I cannot but think there was every excuse
For Will Abbott, in taking and making the use
He did of the helmet, to prove he had done
All that he engaged in the wager he won.
He was proud of his trophy, and show'd it to many,
And his tale disbelieved was by few, if by any.
But anon it appear'd that a mystical being
Of a kind we are not in the habit of seeing,—
A member of some subterranean society,—
Did not think that bold Will had behaved with propriety.
In the yard of Church Living a very strange sight
Was seen by the village-folk often at night,
A hitherto-never-beheld apparition,
Like a bundle of straw in a state of ignition,
Which sway'd to and fro with a slow restless motion,
As a boat with the ebb and the flow of the ocean.
Seen by *us*, such a weird *oscillation* might bring
Reminiscence, perhaps, of a person call'd *Swing*,

Well, or rather, *ill* known, as the Genius of arson,
Who 'gainst threshing-machines carried igneous wars on.
This terrible sight put the folks in a fright,
As it seem'd to *demon*strate that all was not right:
Especially those in the farm-house who dwelt,
With it close to their doors, much disquietude felt.
And took it to heart to be so incommoded
By a portent which certainly nothing good boded;
And often debated what course was most proper
To put on this dreadful annoyance a stopper.

In order this troublesome matter to settle,
Will Abbott surrender'd the head-piece of metal:
By the parson's advice, it was thrown, like a bowl,
With a strong underhand pitch, far into the hole,
Which was then closed with stones and cement very neatly—
Expedients which answer'd the purpose completely;
For the igneous spectre at once ceased from giving
Disturbance and fright to the folks of Church Living.

I have but to add, that, in corroboration
Of the legend rehearsed in this faithful narration,
A joiner, of late, on the roof newly stripp'd,
Perceived, what before observation had slipp'd,
A small antique chimney that could not be known
Connected with any room, upstairs or down,
Of the farm-house. 'Twas built in an old massive wall:
And when, for the trial of its depth, he let fall
A stone in the opening,—how strange some things are!—
He heard it go rattling down, ever so far!

c

MORAL.

I think it expedient that one, when he's able,
A moral should draw from a story or fable:
And surely the tale which I've told makes it clear
How an enterprise which, at first sight, may appear
Full of risk, and the mind with vague terror may fill,
Is achieved very soon by a resolute *Will*.
But it follows not hence that they merit our praise,
Who heedlessly venture in dark ugly ways;
Especially when they're unable to plead
That a question exists as to whither they lead.
A course of this nature, whoever may try it,
Will usually cause him alarm and disquiet.
And the legend assures us of no lasting gain
From such ways, or the things that to them appertain.
Also Prudence suggests, as by far the best plan,
That we close their dark entries as soon as we can:
Since to those who've explored them it ought to be plain
That nothing should tempt them to venture again.

THE SPECTRAL HORSEWOMAN.

'He carries weight! he rides—'
The Ballad of John Gilpin.

THE farm-house clock strikes twelve at last;
It strikes the hour a quarter too fast:
And the farmer mutters ' She'll be here soon,—
The troublesome creature that comes at noon ;
But I've ask'd Parson Hewitt to come to-day,
And do what he can to put her away.
N.B. Understand that to ' put away,'
When applied to a ghost, is the same as ' to lay.'

Look in the court! What see you there?
A veritable *Fille-de-l'Air* ;
A steed all ghost from head to tail,
By the ghost of a bridle tied to a rail.
The more you look, it is apparent
That the grey is strikingly transparent ;—
A most *mysterious* thing to view,
Yet very easily *seen through.*

But where is the horsewoman clothed in white,
Who hither comes in the broad day-light,
Unghostlike preferring the day to night?
Having fasten'd her steed,—that mysterious grey,—
To the gate of the yard, in the usual way,
Like a meteor o'er the marish fleeting,
Like a morning mist from the vale retreating,
Or, in other words, 'as still as a mouse,'
She went up the stairs of the old farm-house
To a room where she sits in loneliness
For half an hour, be it more or less;
And then down again will she noiselessly steal,
While the farm-folk are taking their mid-day meal,
And with them sit for another half hour,—
No welcome guest; but 'tis past their power
To make her depart: it is proved to be quite,
Quite useless to try to 'walk into' a sprite,
In a physical sense. One may sit on the chair,
Or the bench, where she's seen; but as soon as he's there
At once she appears in a different place.
They may talk as they please; they may jeer in her face;—
Her face so fix'd and pale the while,
With never a frown, and never a smile;
They may raise a loud laugh or obstreperous shout;
But they can in no sense of words, 'put her out';
For one may as well run his head 'gainst a post
As in this skilless manner contend with a ghost.
Full glad will the farm-people be, I count,
When they see that spectral woman remount

Her phantom steed. The high-way flint
Will be silent beneath the seeming dint
Of those shadowy hoofs, while the ghostly grey
By the road down the hill shall take its way,
Soon to vanish in air, to the far spirit-clime
Fleeting back, not on earth to be seen till next time.

Suppose then the spectre, as is her wont,
Having gone upstairs to a room in the front
Of the house, to be sitting all lonely there,
While the folks in the kitchen are quite aware
Of her session above, and the steed at the gate;
And think it a most disagreeable state
Of things; for 'tis perfectly understood
By the veriest child that she comes for no good;
And none's pleased with the thought that ere long she will be
For about half an hour in their company:
And the farmer mutters, 'My best rick of hay
I'd give for the power to put her away':—
At this crisis, the sound of a horse trotting hard
Is heard; but is stopp'd at the gate of the yard;
And the sight of the parson upon his stout cob
Makes every heart with excitement to throb.
An orthodox parson he is, every inch,—
Not one who from ghost or from demon would flinch;
And who knows those strange words which are fit to be said
To a ghost, who in Latin is always well-read.

The farmer likes well the appearance of Hewitt,
And says *sotto voce*, 'I guess he can do it.'

From the window he goes to the doorway, and meets
The divine, whom he thus in an undertone greets,
With finger on lip, and mysterious airs,
' You're come at the right time;—but, hush! she's upstairs;
Will you go up? She'll be in the kitchen bime-bye.'
' Better see her at once,' was the parson's reply:
But just as his foot on the first step he set,
The spectre descending he suddenly met.
There was no time to lose: so without more ado,
With a broadside of Latin he made her bring to;
'Adjuro te ut dicas mihi
Cur, spiritus, meridici
Huc venis tam frequenter hora:
Responde mihi sine mora.'

Then first the sprite, who never was heard
Before to utter a single word,
Replied in low mysterious tones,
Like the night-wind's faint sighing moans:
I only say, ' like them'; for this earth
To such strange tones gave never birth,
Tones of the far-off spirit-clime,
Beyond the brawling stream of Time.
Whatever it was she was heard to speak,
The farmer profess'd that to him it was Greek:
But the answer which his adjuration had wrung
From the ghost, Hewitt said, was in his mother-tongue.
Then, as though his address and demeanour commanding
Had effected between them a good understanding,

The ghost follow'd Hewitt out into the court,
Where—not to concoct a long tale of a short—
He mounted his cob, she her shadowy grey ;
And parson and ghost side by side rode away
Down the hill : the farm-people rush out eager-eyed
To see all they can of this marvellous ride.

The parson and ghost both together still fare,—
The cob neck-and-neck with the tall *Fille-de-l'Air*.
For a moment they're lost at the foot of the hill ;
But, beyond, they're again seen in company still.
At the cross-road that very mysterious grey
To the gate of a steep tillage-field turns away :
Through that steep field they pass, and two others, and
    now
Together are seen on the hill's grassy brow ;
Then descending the opposite side disappear
From the eyes of the gazers who watch their career.

I believe it was never precisely related
How the ghost from the parson at last separated ;
But the latter reach'd home in good time and all right,
Having been most successful in laying the sprite ;
Which never again at the farm-house, I wis,
Has made its appearance from that time to this.
But of what Hewitt learnt from his free conversation
With her, during the ride, I may here make relation.
She told him that during her mortal existence
She in service domestic had earn'd her subsistence ;

But latterly came to this farm to abide
For awhile; and was there seized with sickness, and died.
And the reason she gave for her haunting of late
The farm-house was, that she'd made free with some plate,
While in her last place, which she managed to hide
In the tick of the bed in the room where she died.
When he ask'd her what room 'twas, she answer'd, ' That
      is it
To which upstairs I went when I came on my visit.'
She said that it caused her no little vexation
That so long time she could not afford information;
' For one must not,' she said, ' any spirit expect
To speak until question'd in manner correct.'
She remark'd, too, that she'd be no longer constrain'd
To visit the house now that all was explain'd.

And now, gentle reader, the whole that is left
To relate is, that proof soon appear'd of the theft.
Acting on information received from the sprite,
The bed tick they ripp'd, when some spoons came to light.
Now I cannot assert that I ever yet learn'd
That the plate to the owner was duly return'd.
I, however, suppose he regain'd what he lost:
If he did not, it was not the fault of the ghost,
Who enjoin'd its return; denounced all who should let it;
And repeatedly said that she wished he might get it.

PIXY-LED.

' Mislead night-wanderers, laughing at their harm.'

Midsummer Night's Dream.

THOMAS PARKER came of a Devonshire strain ;
His habits were simple ; his habit was plain ;
A long-skirted coat he was wont to wear,
Which gave him rather a rustified air ;
Thanks to his wife's needle, it always look'd neat,
Although of a pattern quite obsolete.
It had long flapp'd pockets, wherein he stow'd
Of household stores the requisite load,
Whene'er, by a footpath much cumber'd with stiles,
He went from his house to the town—full two miles.

One afternoon—'twas in September,
As many a gossip could long remember,
He started on his accustom'd route—
'Twas the shortest one could go by foot.
The path lay close along a brook,
Which flow'd in many a pleasing nook ;

Here, beneath knots of alders, darkling,
There, in a deep eddy gushing and sparkling;
Here, babbling 'gainst a stony beach;
There, shining in an open reach,
Dimpled by spotted trout that rise
Eager to take the gauze-wing'd flies.
With here and there upon its brink
A flush of flowers, purple or pink;
Splendour of lythrum and pale willow-herb,
In their autumnal bloom superb;
Water-flags, kexes, and nettles, and thistles
With leaves terminating in sharp-pointed bristles;
Reeds, rushes, and carnation-grass,
Imaged within the lucent glass;
Broad-leaved docks, and mint, and mallows,
And cresses that love to run into the shallows;
And plants which I can't well describe, having not any
Very extensive acquaintance with botany.
This fringe the mower's scythe had left,
When of its crop the field it reft.

He reach'd the town, and the requisites bought,
With which his coat-pockets were duly fraught.
It is not needful to my story
That I should give an inventory
Of all his stock—'tis my intention
Of but one article to make mention,
Viz., a pound of candles call'd dips,
Which he usually fetch'd in these afternoon trips.

This parcel, moreover, I'd have you take note,
He placed in a poke of the long-skirted coat.
Then he went to the Crown, where for some time he stay'd,
By which his return was a little delay'd.
Ere the clock had struck nine he set out on his way.
But, somehow, he did not reach home till next day;
Nor did he return by the way that he came;
For which, ever after, the Pixies he'd blame—
An excuse which some folks would denominate 'lame.'
'Twas strange that a man who most times acted warily,
Should out of his way have gone involuntarily,
And taken a course in great measure contrarily.
But to solve this enigma 'twill doubtless avail
To hear Thomas Parker relate his own tale.

T. P.'s NARRATIVE.

I done mee arrands at the town,
An' vor an hour or zo zot down,
And drink'd a pint o' ale at the Crown;
An whan I leaved, 'twere jist about nine;
The night simm'd likely to be vine.
It warnt auver dark nor 'twarnt auver light,
An' I took'd the sdtile, as I dthought, quit right.
Zo I guess'd I wur in the reglar track
That 'ud bring me to mee huome striaght back.
Zo on I goed, till the way simm'd queare;
An' I couldn't vine I wur gitting neare
Mee journey's eend; but I sdtill walk'd spry,
Thof the way simm'd straange-like; and bime-bye

Mee 'ead wur all ov a zweamy zwim,
And mee eyes bekimm'd inkimminly dim.
Zumow, vor sartin, mee way I'd a-lost;
An' I can't a bit zay what viels I cross'd,
Clamb'ring droo adges, auver vences,
Lik wan vorzaken ov 'is zenses.
Zo many a weary hour I 'vared,
Dizzy-eaded, a-tired, and a-skear'd;
'Till I recauver'd zense to dthink
That I warn't the wuss vor a drap o' drink,
Whik voke mid zay 'ad got in mee 'ead,
But dthat I wur sartinly Pixy-led.
Zo I turn'd mee pocket inzide-out,
An' immadiately know'd mee whereabout:
In Edge coort-yard meezelf I persayved;
I wur rayther zurprised, but mee mind wur ralayved;
Vive long mile an' a 'alf I'd a-come;
Jist as var vrom the town as I wur from mee huome.
Zo I turn'd about, an' walk'd quit striaght
Untill I comm'd to mee awn coort-giate,
As well's a ever zince I began
To walk; or any other man.
Well! 'twur a pracious rig I rañ,
Whan I wur dthic evenin' Pixy-led,
And wan holl night kep out o' mee bed:
And I gueess 'twur a most partiklar thing,
That arter this here wandering,
Mee passel wur zafe within mee poke,
And not a zingle candle a-broke.

MORAL.

Without harshly judging this Devonshire yeoman,
It should ne'ertheless be forgotten by no man,
That the sprites who the spirit-king, Alcohol, serve,
Do oft from his path make the way-farer swerve.
Then let all honest swains who would keep the right way,
Beware how they bring themselves under their sway;
For the legs will be prone to take any direction,
When the head is deprived of its power of reflection.

THE FAST-GROWING PIG.

' Which, no doubt,
Grew, like the summer-grass, fastest by night.'

SHAKSPEARE.

I QUESTION if ever you heard of a pig
That grew in a short time so monstrously big
As that very remarkable porker, the rate
Of whose increase I am now about to relate.
'Twas at the close of an autumn day,
That two young lace-makers took their way
Up a rather steep hill from the village of B——,
That lies in a vale of the West, by the sea:—
Mary Jane, Sarah Ann—names quite common among
The lace-girls:—their short patronymic was Long.
One day every week to this village they brought
The lace which at home, five miles distant, they wrought.
Now homeward returning, with various chat
Their way they beguiled, about this thing and that.
The shades of night deepen'd as onward they went;
And they'd just gain'd the top of that steep hill's ascent:

When one to the other said, 'O Mary Jane,
I shall feel a bit skear'd, going through Bovey Lane.
Haven't ee heard of the *thing* that wur seen t'other night.
And put Butcher Drake and his horse in a vright?
A zed it wur just like a gert zack o' wool,
And roll'd in a way that wur quite wonderful
Down the hedge just avore en, and right 'cross the road,
And up opposite hedge like a living thing goed.
Butcher Drake zed he couldn't tell what to make on't;
But Farmer Pike zeth that, vor his part, he don't
Doubt 'tis the ghost of an ole Chanc'ry suit[1]
'Bout Bovey estate,—he's a man that be cute:
And a zeth, "If it be, I can tell em,—iss, fay[2]!
They'll find it a tough job to put en away."'

These words were scarce spoken, when Sarah Ann
Look'd back, and was ware that behind them ran
A little pig of a swarthy hue,
With his small eye fix'd on the sisters two.
They laugh'd, as they look'd at the queer little pig.
Who seem'd very knowing, although far from big.
Their talk they resumed, and still kept on their way,
Now on grave things discoursing, and now upon gay;
When Mary Jane turn'd, and saw very near
The porker following in the rear,
Considerably increased in size;—
She hardly could believe her eyes.

---

[1] An inference drawn from the known connection between the Lord Chancellor and woolsack.
[2] Yes, in faith!

'Look, Sarah Ann! the pig just now
Zo zmall, is quite as big's a zow;
And blacker than a was avore;
It ain't a real pig I'm zhure.'

The girls were then in an awful state:
Their hearts began to palpitate:
Their footsteps trembled as in haste
Along the darkling road they paced.
So much did fright oppress each mind,
Some time they durst not look behind;
But one glimpsed back, at Sandy Hollow,
To see if still the pig did follow;
And screaming cried, 'He's more nor half
As big again!—'s like a gert calf!'

This seeming anything but fun,
The maidens both began to run;
Never once looking back, but squalling,
And with loud cries for succour calling.
Thus flying, like a partridge covey,
They pass the entrance-road to Bovey;
Then from the bye-way they diverge,
And on the main high road emerge;
And soon they see—most welcome sight!—
A roadside cottage, 'Stoford' hight,
One Milton lived there with his dame.
Thither the frighted maidens came,

And roused the couple from repose
With cries for help that loudly rose.
'O Mrs. Milton, do come down,
And let us in.' 'Go home to town,
Ye hollering bold jades,' Milton said,
'A-startling vokes that be in bed.'
But his missis, who—lucky for them!—was possess'd
Of a kind heart, was moved by the maidens' distress;
Rose from bed, donn'd some garments, descended the stair,
And let in the panting and terrified pair.
But ere the good woman the door closed again,
She look'd 'long the road, and beheld very plain
A monster whose aspect with fear chill'd her soul,
As big as a bullock, and black as a coal.

THE BRANSCOMBE FAIRY.

'Heavens defend me from that *Welsh* fairy!'
Falstaff.

BRANSCOMBE lies on the Devonshire coast,
A village celebrated most
For deftly manufactured lace,
Wrought by the lasses of the place ;
And also for potatoes fine
Grown on the seaward cliffs' incline :
'Full of coombes and valleys,' as Risdon says,
Which occasion the steepness of its ways.
Moreover, the parish is possess'd
Of an object of some interest,—
The mansion where dwelt the worthy pair
Who, having no child to be their heir,
Founded, for furtherance of knowledge,
In Oxford city, Wadham College.
Also, the rugged cliffs by the sea
Are said to have harbour'd formerly
A number of people who had turn'd out
To see what Monmouth was about,

When he landed at Lyme, having wrongly reckon'd
That he could oust King James the Second.
When the duke had been worsted, these people lay
In their hollow recesses many a day,
Fearing lest Feversham, or Kirke,
With them, if caught, might make short work;
Or Jefferies, the judge with the truculent eyes,
Should have them arraign'd at his Bloody Assize,
Where jurymen could only find
One verdict suited to the mind
Of the savage judge whose brutal rage
Has foully stain'd our history's page;
And whose severe unpitying *fiat*
Humanity was forced to sigh at.

In sooth, it was a perilous time,
When curiosity was a crime;
And some were not allow'd to live
For being too inquisitive;
Although they'd done no more than run
To see what they thoughtlessly call'd 'the fun.'

Looking seaward, one sees on the left
Of Branscombe Mouth's wide-riven cleft,
Which gives to three deep vales a view
Of the Channel's wandering fields of blue,
A farm-house built on a pleasant site,
Where the hill slants back from the cliff's steep height;

Overblown by the soft sea-wind,
With bowery orchards close behind ;
An old thatch'd house, with homestead wide,
And a lane in front, and a road at the side.
Overlooking the valley and rill,
So snugly it lies in the bend of the hill,
That for air of repose and rural charm
(As George Robins[1] might say, whose descriptions were
    warm),
One can see few places like Sea-side Farm.

Here I am come to the scene of my story.
The details I'll now set before ye.

But, first of all, I must premise
To those who might else my tale despise,
That 'tis by no means fabricated,
But a story well authenticated ;
For the wonder, which I now make bold
To relate, was a great many years ago told
To the oldest inhabitant's father, who heard
From the witness the narrative, every word.

The witness lived at Sea-side Farm :
There was never report of any harm

---

[1] The auctioneer.

Of him or his; but 'twas his fate,
One night, when home returning late,
To find a most unusual prize,
Which fill'd him with immense surprise;
In short, a windfall most uncommon,—
A very pretty little woman :
But that was not so great a wonder,
As how much the average height she was under,
Being only six inches high, a creature
Perfect in form, and lovely in feature ;
Drest in green,—a fairy, no doubt,
As far as we know aught about
Those airy beings who, tales agree,
Oft dance by night on the moonlit lea.

But, hold! methinks I hear one say
That man is compacted of bibulous clay;
And that all objects far less clear
By moonlight, than by day, appear.
But he always averr'd that he made no mistake,
Being perfectly sober, and wide-awake ;
And the sequel, according as he it related,
Dispels such base doubt insinuated ;
And seems all question to allay
About its being a genuine fay.
Moreover, he always most sensibly said,
' How could such a thing have come into my head?'
And surely one well may suppose that a swain,
Whose manner of living and thinking is plain,

Is not very capable of a romantic
Invention like that of a poet half-frantic.
Mayhap he would have been nothing loth
To take his 'davy [1],' or bible-oath,
If it had been required, in attestation
Of the truth of his asseveration.
And if any suggest that my hero was mad,
Which would make the deception not morally bad,
I believe I may state that he'd no more insanity
Than belongs to the usual lot of humanity.

He not only found the fairy, but caught her;
And, highly elated, home he brought her.

He roused his good-woman from her sleep
With a noise that 'struck her all of a heap,'
Blessing his stars for the lucky chance;
In fact, for joy he was ready to dance.
The good-woman cried, 'Why, what's the matter,
That ye come home making such a clatter?'
'I've found the prettiest little woman,—
A treasure I would yield to no man.
What shall I do with the prize I've got?
Lose her for all the world I would not.'
The drowsy good-wife merely said,
Slightly jerking her night-capp'd head,

---

[1] To make affidavit.

' If you would have your luck to last,
Tie her to the bed-post fast ;
Take your garter, tie her tight ;
There let her bide until daylight.'

The fairy to the post made fast,
He went to bed, and there forecast
Full many schemes, elate with rapture
By reason of the fairy's capture.
On one thing he made up his mind,
Which was, to keep her close confined
Until such time as she'd agree
To pay his price for her liberty.
And while thus brooding o'er his schemes,
He fell asleep, and in his dreams
Saw Fairy-land, and all its treasure
Of gold and silver without measure.

When he awoke, his first reflection
Was the very agreeable recollection
Of his lucky catch ; and as soon as 'twas light
He got up to see if all was right,
Hoping the fairy would still be found
At the post, in the garter by which she was bound.

Alack, and alas, for human schemes
Seldom to be fulfill'd as one deems !

There was the post, and the garter too,
That long-worn garter which well he knew:
The knot all right, the identical knot;
But in the garter the fairy was not:
Like a soldier averse from becoming a ghost,
She had surreptitiously left her post.
Alas, for Fortune's whimsical freak!
The garter contained but a good-sized leek.

Great was the farmer's consternation,
So cheated of his expectation;
And he cried, as soon as he could speak,
'The little woman's turn'd into a leek!'
The dame replied: 'Next time you come
Bringing a fairy at midnight home,
And making a row, let your eye-sight' be clear,
And your brains neither muddled with cider nor beer.'

The farmer heard with indignation
The well-meaning woman's objurgation,
And still declared he had not been deceived,
Whether he should or should not be believed;
And having donn'd his clothes, he took
The leek in his hand, with a rueful look;
Crest-fall'n, and flabbergasted quite,
At the very disappointing sight;
Went down the stairs, and open'd the door,

And having look'd it thoroughly o'er,
And seen 'twas a leek and nothing more;
Like Peter Bell's primrose [1], by the brim
Of a river, which was nothing more to him
Than a yellow primrose, he threw it away.
But what was his wonder! how great his dismay!
When he saw, as soon as it touch'd the ground,
That it sprang up at once with a sudden bound,—
The fairy that he had the night before seen,
Drest in a robe of appropriate green;
The same little beautiful woman, a creature
Perfect in form, and lovely in feature.
But another wonder was yet in store;
For as soon as the leek was a fairy once more,
A troop of other little creatures,
Resembling her in height and features,
More than could by the farmer be counted,
Came, all on tiny coursers mounted,
All their bits and bridles jingling,
All their voices in chorus mingling,
As they joyfully shriek'd with might and main,
'We've got her again! we've got her again!'

It is not thought that the cheated wight
Was very much overjoy'd at the sight;

[1] 'A primrose by a river's brim
A yellow primrose was to him,
And it was nothing more.'
WORDSWORTH.

However he may have felt surprise
To find that the leek was a fay in disguise.
The circumstances of the loss,
By which his gold was turn'd to dross,
He told his wife : the strange tale she
Made known in the vicinity.

I know that some will yet raise a doubt
And say, ' To be sure, the drunken lout,
To save his credit for sobriety,
This story palm'd upon society;
Or even allowing his sober condition,
This tale was no less a most gross imposition.

Sceptics, the *onus* rests with you
To prove the tale I've told untrue,
And that the wight had more sagacity,
Or more invention, than veracity;
Or that he was under an hallucination
From drink or mental alienation.
I've told the tale as to me it was told
In the birthplace of the legend old;
And lest some should no moral spy,
I'll do my best one to supply.

MORAL.

In this up-and-down world if you chance to find
A nice little fairy just to your mind,
Don't suddenly change your opinion about her,
And think you are licensed to scorn her and flout her;
Merely because you expected too much,
And your fairy not always appears to be such
As she seem'd to your eyes, when you saw her at first;
For fays have their best looks, and also their worst.

THE FAIRY-RIDDEN HORSE.

' A horse ! a horse !'

Richard III.

THE farmer leant upon a rail,
Viewing his horse from head to tail
With a look of concern; for never before
Had that horse appear'd so lean and poor :
His eyes were dull, and his once sleek coat
Was as rough as the back of a mountain goat :
And he hobbled along like an old cab-hack,
Whose constitution is gone to wrack,
From under-feeding and over-driving,
Which effectually keep a beast from thriving.
That horse, which of late, so lively and sound,
Would have fetch'd no less than twenty pound,
Was now become so dreadfully thin,
That every bone could be seen in his skin ;
Indeed, he was as thin almost
As that apparition call'd a ghost.

The farmer whistled, and shut one eye,
And look'd uncommon knowingly ;

Then, with a judicial shake of his head,
'He's been bewitch'd,' he musingly said :
'Conjurer Baker is the man
To take off the spell, if any one can.'

At once he sent a lad some distance
To ask the conjurer's assistance,
And beg that he would not delay,
As the business was pressing, to come his way.

The conjurer was found at home,
And said he would directly come ;—
A knowing man attired in black,
In the style of those doctors whose prefix is 'Quack.'
More knowing still he look'd anon,
When he put his silver-rimm'd spectacles on,
And took a scientific sight
Of the horse that was in such a woeful plight.
He look'd at him well, and he look'd at him nearly;
And then he said, 'It is most clearly
A case of witchcraft; but I'll be bound
Within a week to make him sound
As any horse the whole country round.'

Forthwith, the conjurer there and then
Agreed with the farmer for two pound ten,
In present payment, to restore
The horse to the state he was in before.
The spell was against his well-being directed
By some cross old hag, as the farmer suspected.

But all in vain was each counter-charm
That the conjurer used, to remove the harm
Which the beast had met with, nor could he dispel
What seem'd a most malignant spell:
So, after a month, to the farmer he said,
'I ne'er had to do with a spell so deep-laid:
'Tis certain the old woman knows well her trade:
However, I've employ'd the best
Of all the skill by me possess'd:
And as for the trifling compensation
You gave me, it is but fair remuneration
For the trouble I've taken, and risk I have run,
In what 'gainst the powers of darkness I've done.'
So the farmer, looking rather funny [1],
Agreed that he had earn'd the money.

The honest farmer, rather perplex'd,
After debating what he should do next,
Resolved on a scheme less visionary,
And sent for a surgeon veterinary;
A red-whisker'd man who wore gaiters drab,
And among his gifts number'd 'the gift of the gab.'
He came, and survey'd the unfortunate horse,
Which seem'd very near being changed to a corse;
And first having made the poor farmer endure
The recital of many a wonderful cure,
Set to work with drench and bolus strong;
But was forced to give it up ere long,

[1] Disconcerted.

Saying, 'I count your horse gets thinner:
He don't look like the Derby winner;
And I really think that he'll die of the phthisic.
Will you settle the bill for attendance and physic?'

The farmer was now obliged, perforce,
To let the matter take its course;
And leave it to Nature to determine
How soon the horse should be food for vermin.
But, lo! all at once the hidden mystery
Involved within this little history,
Was quite clear'd up by a labourer's means,
Who went a-field, before the beams
Of Phoebus had illumined the skies:
I know not what made him so early to rise;
What time the dull grey morn first broke,
And the valley was full of a mist white as smoke;
And the meadow's green of sullen hue
Was wrapt in shade, and heavy with dew.
As through the field he chanced to pass,
Where he thought that the invalid horse was at grass,
He look'd around, but no horse could he see;
So he stood and wonder'd where he could be.
And, at last, after stopping awhile, he spied
Coming in, by a gate at the field's farther side,
The missing horse, from a nightly excursion,
Which it seems had afforded the fairies diversion:
For the beast by a number of fairies was driven:
With such treatment no wonder that he had not thriven.

Some of the fairies were goading his flanks
With a vehemence scarcely deserving his thanks;
Some by his tail held on and swung;
Some on his back to and fro themselves flung;
One on each ear was perch'd; some of the train
Sat on his neck, tying knots in his mane.
That their tricks had distress'd him 'twas easy to gather
From the foam on his mouth, and his sides in a lather.
But as soon as they saw that their pranks were espied,
With a sudden shriek, away they all hied.

I know not whether the legend says
That they rode the poor horse to the end of his days;
Or whether—as fairies are rather shy
Of their sports being witness'd by mortal eye—
They abstain'd for the future from teasing the beast,
Whence his health was restored, and his bulk was increased:
I know not;—and 'tis no great matter;
Though I fain would believe that the case was the latter.

MORAL.

Whatever the ailment you have to endure,
You scarcely can hope to experience its cure
By a doctor who's not free from quackery's taint,
And treats, when he can't diagnose, your complaint.

A SALISBURY GHOST STORY.

'Let me have no intruder.'
SHAKSPEARE.

A METHOD consider'd effective, though mild,
In dealing with any refractory child,
Is this,—that, instead of inflicting a beating
(Which, however, is sometimes the best way of treating
A boy, who is gifted with feelings less tender
Than belong to a child of the feminine gender),
You should presently seize the refractory elf,
And in a room place it apart by itself,
Either upstairs or downstairs, an hour to remain,—
A room in which silence and solitude reign;
And if there be added a *quantum* of gloom,
I should say, 'So much better for penance the room:'
But black utter darkness, I think, acts too strongly
On the feelings and nerves of a child who's done wrongly:
And be sure that to stir up a feeling of terror
In a child, is not best for correcting an error.

Now it happen'd with little Elizabeth Carter,
Whose temper was that of a perfect young Tartar,

F.

That having been naughty, she 'd just been consign'd
To a lone still apartment, not much to her mind,
In the hope that such mild and judicious correction
Would abate her self-will and give time for reflection.
Shoeless, laid on a bed (to remove shoes is laudable;
It renders both stamping and kicking less audible),
She had had a good cry, out of spite and vexation,
Which is oft the first fruit of an incarceration,
That makes a child feel rather put on its mettle,
Before there is time for the feelings to settle;
And was now just becoming a little subdued,
And inclined to a more satisfactory mood,
When something occurr'd,—'twas a wonder most strange,—
A something quite out of the usual range
Of the various events which are wont to befall
Men or children on this our terrestrial ball.

She saw the door open, and enter a figure,
To her apprehension as dire as a nigger,
A man in knee-breeches attired, and long coat,
And long flower'd waistcoat, as well she could note.
On his shoes there were buckles, and eke at his knees;
But the former the largest by many degrees.
On his head was a queer hat, which most made her stare,
Three-corner'd, gold-laced, quite à la militaire.

Now Bessie, of course, had she happen'd to know
What costumes prevail'd in times not long ago,
Might have fancied this one of those old Salamanders
Who in Dutch William's time, or in Anne's, fought in
    Flanders:

Or, otherwise, might with some reason have reckon'd
Him a gentleman *temp*. George the First, or the Second:
But being entirely unskill'd in all lore
Respecting the dresses our ancestors wore;
And ne'er having seen deck'd in raiment so garish
Any one save the Beadle,—that gem of her parish,—
Named King,—a great bugbear to all the small folk,
To whom, though, of course, it was only in joke,
Their temper-tried mothers, to scare them, would say,
'The Beadle shall come, and he'll take you away,'
She supposed, as for her was a natural thing,
That this was the said Beadle, *nomine* King.

Then said little Bess, who was frighten'd completely,
'I hope, Mr. King, you're not going to beat me':
But the quaint person only agreeably smiled,
As he came near the bed, and regarded the child.
Then, turning away, as the window he near'd,
He all in a jiffy, or wink, disappear'd:
And the child, thinking that he had suddenly gone
By a fall from the window the hard ground upon,
Which had badly 'caved in' his respectable pate,
Began to lament the supposed Beadle's fate.
'Oh, dear! oh, dear! oh, poor Mr. King!
He's certainly dead! what a terrible thing!'
But when to the window she ran, and look'd out,
She perceived he had managed his *exit* without
Such catastrophe; for she saw nothing at all,
Where she thought she should view the result of the fall.

As soon as the term of her penance was o'er,
And the promise was made to be naughty no more,
She gave a narration of what she had seen,
While alone by herself in the room she had been.
But her mother, though thinking that she'd chanced to
    see a
Real ghost, did not wish to disturb the idea
In the mind of the child, that the Bumble familiar
It was who this visit had paid domiciliar.
But when Bess by several years had grown older,
Her mother, without any more scruple, told her
That in this same house long ago there resided
A curious old gentleman, amply provided
With monies and chattels, whose nephew and heir,—
One who with George Barnwell might very well pair,—
Although of his counsels extremely unheedful,
Expected him always to furnish 'the needful':
As indeed it is usual for one who is 'flash'
To look to 'his uncle' to keep him in cash.

After wandering about in a rather wild way,
This nephew return'd to his uncle's one day;
And thinking it rather too tedious to wait
Till he came in due course to the old man's estate ;
Or else being under disquietude lest
His relation might choose to revoke his bequest ;
All agape for his wealth, like a greedy young gudgeon,
With pistol, knife, handkerchief, poison, or bludgeon,
He, 'tis said, made away with the poor old curmudgeon,
Who at his ill deeds had oft been in high dudgeon.

The uncle, since then, as misliking his ' clearance,'
Had been known at odd times to ' put in an appearance'
In the very same chamber where little Miss Bess
Was consign'd for an hour to a lonely *duresse*;
And which was, it seems, the identical one
In which the foul deed by the nephew was done.
How the nephew 'scaped hanging does not quite appear;
But it seems that the proof of his guilt was not clear;
And so, like some others who follow such ways,
He eluded Jack Ketch to the end of his days.

In short, then, the upshot of this tale is,
That no *Scarabaeus Parochialis*,
As the Parish Beadle hath been named
By Thomas Hood, the jester famed,
But a genuine ghost had appear'd in the room,
Where the poor old gentleman met with his doom.

THE ODSTOCK GIPSY.

' He stutter'd o'er blessing, he stutter'd o'er ban,
  He stutter'd drunk or dry,
And none but he and the fisherman
  Could tell the reason why.'
                    PRAED, *The Red Fisherman.*

THAT 'the Gipsy life is a joyous life,'
  Hath been both sung and said.
To live in a tent without paying house-rent,
  And not to work *hard* for your bread,
Are pleasant, when you have not to plague you,
Rheumatism, neuralgia, or ague.

But not without shades is the gipsy's life ;
And it's not altogether so free from strife
    As song-writers it portray :
Besides, the gipsy's a bit of a rake ;
And he's also given to make a mistake,
    And unscrupulous hands to lay
On the 'things' and the 'beasts' which belong to another ;
And this makes it hard our conviction to smother,

That though he can dance, and drink, and fight
Equally well by moon- and sun-light,
The 'ranting rollicking Romany'
Is up to more tricks than he ought to be.

A gipsy there was, named Joshua Shemp,
Who flourish'd *Georgii Tertii temp.*:
Little is of his aspect known
From what report has handed down.
We may suppose him to have been
A gipsy of no common mien ;
Whether of easy *dégagée* air,
Or with look of reserve and gloomy care ;
Both of which types of face we see
In the gipsy's wild society ;
Owning a dark-eyed olive-hued wife,
And leading the regular gipsy life ;
True to his word, and true to his friend ;
Of courage firm, which nought could bend ;
In short, a haunter of forest and fen
Who was one of Nature's own gentlemen.

I once heard 'a party' in a train,
His idea of a gentleman thus explain :
'I don't mean a fellow,' he went on to say,
'Who eats salmon and lobster-sauce every day,
        But a fellow who 's right inside.'
And I think that we often may detect
In the lowliest peasant that self-respect,—
        That feeling of proper pride,

Which is, in fact, the very backbone
Of a mind of gentlemanly tone.

In the very first year of this century's course,
Joshua was charged with stealing a horse.
To the parish constables then in vogue
Was committed the task of arresting a rogue.
Somehow or other, they managed to do
Without the police, in comparison, new.
So one fine day, in a woodland nook,
They seized him, and to prison took,
To stand his trial at the assizes
Held at Salisbury,—*not* at Devizes.
Witnesses were produced who swore
To all they knew, and, perhaps, something more:
The jury, rightly, as they thought,
In their verdict of 'guilty' brought;
And the judge pronounced the sentence dread,
That Shemp should be hang'd until thrice-dead,
Adding a prayer,—'tis the usual *rôle*,—
That the Lord might have mercy on his soul;
Supposed to be kindly meant, for the sake
Of the culprit, as though intended to make
The sentence easier of digestion,
Mercy from man being out of the question.

I doubt if ever the world has heard
Of harsher laws than those in force
In the blissful reign of George the Third,
When a man could be hang'd for stealing a horse.

I think we shall never have again
Such *capital* laws as old England had then.
Burglars, sheepstealers, knights of the road,
Suffer'd alike by that barbarous code.
One-pound-note forgers expiated
Their fault by being strangulated.
But now the laws are alter'd quite,
And that rarity, hanging, is shrouded from sight:
And a rogue envelop'd in Fraud's own hood,
   Of their store may the widow and orphan bereave,
And be sentenced to penal servitude,
   Soon to get free on a ticket of leave.

But it seems, after all, that the British Themis
Had drawn her conclusion from a wrong premiss;
Or that, in plain English, there was a flaw
In these proceedings of the law
In Joshua's case; for, to be brief,
He was not, they say, the real horse-thief;
But his son-in-law was the man who had taken
The horse, and then wanted 'to save his own bacon.'

For certain reasons that Joshua had,
He made up his mind not to peach on the lad:
It might have been out of consideration
For his daughter, and her young population;
Or for the youthful years of the boy,
And the many more that he might enjoy:
Whereas he himself, being fifty years old,
Had seen all the flower of his life unfold;

And even with those who live in clover
The best part of life, by fifty, is over.
Protesting his innocence to the last,
This resolution he still held fast.
By whatever motives he was sway'd,
'Twas a gallant resolve that the gipsy made.

Joshua Shemp, then, as heroic
Almost as a martyr, and quite as a Stoic,
Bravely underwent his fate:
And when the gallows had done its part
   (Thus I have heard them tell the tale),
His corpse was brought by the gipsies' cart
   From the scaffold in front of New Sarum's gaol
To Odstock, where it lay in state
For the space of a week,—so his friends decreed,
As an honour of stedfast courage the meed.
The older inhabitants show the place still,
By the road at the foot of Odstock Hill,
Between two bridges spanning a bourn
That flows from the Naiad Ebele's urn;
Part in its old accustom'd bed,
Part by a newer channel led.
The wither'd stump of a dead ash-tree
Marks the place where they laid out the Romany,
Looking as though it had vainly tried
To live where the body lay in state
Of the gipsy wight who so hardily died,
As the villagers one and all relate.

The gipsy's corpse was afterwards laid
In a grave in Odstock churchyard made ;
And a stone was placed, with an inscription
Which of name, age, and date of death, gives description ;
But does not describe the particular kind
Of fate to which nobly himself he resign'd :
The letters of which still well endure,
Since they are, in French phrase, *taillées d'une main sûre:*
And it may be inferr'd that to death he was done
On April the first, eighteen hundred and one.
At the top is an hour-glass which typifies sadly
'Brief Life.' The design's executed not badly.

For the sake of conferring a greater distinction
On their *confrère* whose life had thus suffer'd extinction,
They placed about the grave a border
    Of shrubs, with a wooden fence,
Which the sexton agreed to keep in order
    For a yearly amount of pence.
And here it is needful, I think, to remark
That the sexton had also the office of clerk.
Year after year the gipsy race
Held a kind of festival at the place ;
But when the meeting was dropp'd one year,
The cause of which circumstance does not appear,
The parish priest and his churchwarden
Did a thing which the gipsies was rather hard on.
Misliking the rout of the annual feast,
And the kind of ovation they gave the deceased,

They charged the sexton to open out
The grave from the fence which hedged it about;
Which was forthwith done; but the gipsy crew
Came again next year, and made great ado,
On the day of their annual celebration,
At what they considered a desecration :
And a wizen'd, yellow-skinn'd, hollow-eyed crone,
Standing by the revered tombstone,
Duly pronounced a threefold curse,
Which I've made an attempt to render in verse.
'May the farmer (*i.e.* the churchwarden) fail,
And be forced by misfortune his deed to bewail;
May the clerk never do his duty again;
And may the clergyman never speak plain.'
Well, the farmer *was* forced his farm to quit;
And the clerk next sunday *was* seized with a fit,
And carried from church, and never more
Perform'd the duties he 'd done before :
And the parson's curse *was* fulfill'd to the letter,
For he'd previously stutter'd, and never spoke better.

Robert Burns, who was well aware what he was at,
Has declared that a man is a man for a' that;
And a hero 's a hero all the same,
Whether bearing a grand or a humble name :
And long shall we search before we find
Another act of such a kind,—
Another man who the fatal hemp
Would brave for his friend, like Joshua Shemp.

THE HAG IN THE RED CLOAK.

'I saw her but a moment.'
Song.

IT seems quite remarkable how many times
Old women are mentioned in popular rhymes.
 There was an old woman who lived in a shoe,
And with her many children knew not what to do.'
' There was an old woman; and what do you think?
She lived upon nothing but victuals and drink.'
' There was an old woman lived under a hill:
And if she 's not gone, she lives there still.'
' There was an old woman as I've heard tell;
She went to market, her eggs for to sell.'
And we 're told of another remarkable wonder,—
A female,—to whom all the rest must knock under.
' There was an old woman toss'd up in a blanket,
  Seventy times as high as the moon:
   And what she did there
   Oh! nobody knows';—
  But she did not do much,
  We well may suppose;
For,—scarce less remarkable than such a prank,—it
Is said that she came down again *very soon* [1].

[1] N.B. Not the only version.

And now the intelligent reader must own
That I've a good sample of precedents shown
For the use of those words, 'There was an,' &c.;
And surely, if I can't excogitate better a
Beginning than this, no one ought me to blame,
If the words which my tale introduce are the same.
There was an old woman;—a being not rare
Is an elderly female :—the question is, Where?

And here I'm afraid I must make an apology;
For, according to Anthropo- and Physio-logy,
I doubt whether I am permitted to call
My subject a *real* old woman at all;
Being only a ghost, or e'en but a creation
Of the brain, which is due to the mind's aberration:
But whichever view of the phantom we take,
We'll 'an old woman' call it for courtesy's sake.

And now,—to return to the question of 'Where?'—
I think it will rather surprise you to hear
That on the identical Farm she appear'd
Call'd Berry, of which you already have heard,
As the *locus* to which the ghost-story belongs,
About the vile man, and the lady's dire wrongs:
And whether the *thing* were witch, spectre, or fairy,
It was at this farm it was seen in the dairy.

And now, *Exponam eam rem*
Vobis secundum ordinem.

Or, 'In due course I'll set before ye
The circumstances of this story.'
At that remote indefinite
Period, so oft by those who write
Stories in prose, or tales in rhyme,
Referr'd to, 'Once upon a time,'
To Berry came weekly a Wesleyan minister,
With nothing about him that could be term'd sinister;
And, far be it from me,—ay, far as Cape Finisterre,—
To say that he was not what any one can
Describe as a very respectable man.
In short, he was no amateur at his calling,
Whose preaching consists less in sense than in bawling;
But a thorough professional, than whose demeanour
Could nothing be more circumspect, or serener.

It was the custom of this wight
At the Farm-House to pass the night
Of Saturday, and eke of Sunday,
And, after breakfast, leave on Monday.
If I aright the tale remember,
One Monday morning in September,
His temporary lodgings leaving,
He pass'd the dairy, and perceiving
The good-wife there, he likewise view'd
A hag who at her elbow stood,—
A most peculiar old woman,—
As strange a sight as aught that's human;
Accoutred in a cloak of red,
With a peak'd hat upon her head.

He noticed too her high-heel'd shoes,
Such as e'en now the ladies use,
And that she had a walking-staff ;—
The figure wellnigh made him laugh;
And to himself he said, 'I'll learn,
When next I to this house return,
Who this old woman is; for ne'er
Have I beheld a sight so queer.'

Accordingly, when next he came,
He question'd thus the farmer's dame;
'Whom had you in the dairy, pray,
With you, the morn I went away?
For, surely, with you was a creature
Of most unusual garb and feature.'
She answer made; 'Not any one:
I by myself was quite alone.'
This unexpected information
Caused to our friend great consternation;
And thinking that it was unhealthy
To lodge where spectres came so stealthy,
He from that time unto the door
Of Berry Farm-House came no more.

I fear that it is all in vain
To try this mystery to explain.
I've heard that sometimes people see
Strange sights when suffering from *del. tre.*[1];

---

[1] Delirium tremens.

But this man of undoubted piety
Was noted for his strict sobriety :
And while he made this house his quarters,
Was not addicted to strong waters ;
Save that, perchance, one glass he took
Within the farmer's chimney-nook,
On Saturday, or Sunday, night ;
And, sure, that was no more than right.
The fact is, I could ne'er make out it ;
And this is all I know about it.

But, stay ! I can speak of one circumstance more
Which has some relation to what 's gone before :
I have heard it reported that once by the ingle
Of Sea-side Farm-House, which is more than a single
Mile distant from Berry, an old hag was seen ;
And to the belief I confess that I lean,
That she was the same spectre, witch, ghost, or fairy,
Which at Berry the minister saw in the dairy :
For she had a like cloak of red to distinguish her,
And a curious hat in shape like an extinguisher ;
And the like high-heel'd shoes, and a bone-headed staff :—
Altogether, a figure at which you would laugh.
Of the two apparitions this seeming identity
Seems to prove that the old dame was not a non-entity.
And it 's past my ability quite to explain
How the very same phantom of one person's brain,
If the *thing* a mere spectral illusion be reckon'd,
Was impress'd on the optical nerves of a second.

F

It served, they report, not a little to nettle
Farmer Pile, to behold this old hag in his settle;
For not in the least degree felt he delighted
That spirits should come to his house uninvited,
Portending, as he rather thought, some disaster
To the farm-servants, children, or missis, or master;
Or else some occult diabolical harm
To the cows, or the sheep, or the pigs on the farm.
And the not least remarkable circumstance is it
That nothing at all ever came of her visit.

THE BROKEN PILE.

'Palmam qui meruit ferat.'

'Twas on a day long since, I trow,
That a labourer came out to plough
On this hill-side, where from the sea
The breezes come refreshingly,
Heightening the pleasance of the spring
With the ocean-coolness that they bring;
And wafting murmurous dreamy sounds
Of the waves that lave their beachy bounds.

He was a well-conditioned man,
Not given at all to swear, or ban
With imprecations coarse and strong:
But 'Woa!' 'Gee-up!' or 'Come along!'
Unmix'd with aught that good sense shocks,
Was his discourse to horse or ox.

The wind was east, the sky was clear;
'Twas exceedingly hot for the time of the year.
Many a furrow he had turn'd,
Regardless of the sun that burn'd
His face and throat to a brown-red hue,
And sent through every pore a dew.

F 2

Thus while the plough, i' the midst of the field,
Was forcing the stubborn glebe to yield,
(Most strange to tell of!) it occurr'd
That, close behind, a voice he heard
Distinctly say, 'I've broken my pile!'
And here it may be worth the while
To state, for the sake of all those who not duly are
Acquainted with words to the bakers peculiar,
That a pile is a thing by which articles made
For baking are into the oven convey'd.
This voice the swain heard at his back, without seeing
Its owner,—no doubt, a mysterious being:
Its accents were shrill,—such as one would assign
To a female, of temper not over benign.
He heard the voice once; then was silence awhile;
And again was repeated, 'I've broken my pile!'
These words were twice spoken; they may have been thrice;
But the story's not clear in a matter so nice.
Thus spoke the weird voice; the swain stopp'd to per-
    pend it;
Its sense he perceived; and, as soon as he kenn'd it,
This answer return'd, 'Give it me, and I'll mend it.'

In a moment, before him, the pile became visible
(An incident wondrous, and yet almost risible).
As he took it, he said, 'I can understand
That this is a job to be done out of hand:
No doubt, the fairy's oven is hot,
And I must mend it on the spot.'

So, being a very handy swain,
And having his task unmistakeably plain,
He put the broken pile all right,
And made it quite fit for the use of the sprite.
The pile, when set down on the ground, (I'll not blink
The facts of this tale) disappear'd in a wink,
He couldn't tell whither, he couldn't tell how;
And then he went on with his plough.

If this was all, you well might quarrel
With the tale, and say that it wanted a moral.
Not so, gentle reader; the very next day
That labouring man hither took his way,
And found, upon the identical place
Where he left the pile in a better'd case,
A more than ordinary cake,
Such as the fays are accustom'd to make.
'It seems,' he said, ''tis meant to be
Of my small services the fee;
No doubt but it belongs to me:
I'll take possession, which is quite
Nine-tenths, they say, of legal right.'[1]

L'ENVOI.

This story, I take it, proves that elves
Have thoughts in common with ourselves;
And cannot the conviction smother
That 'One good turn deserves another.'

[1] 'Beati possidentes.'

AN AWFUL CHARACTER.

'Monstrum horrendum.'

VIRGIL.

'OH ! Who yon solitary man
That in the bottom's mud
Plunges a pole, and deftly guides
His flat boat through the flood?

'His rigid and mysterious form
Oft have I seen to glide
At one or other of the hours
'Twixt morn and eventide.

'How Charon-like he makes his way,
Though no souls fill his bark.
The business of his life, methinks,
Must be some business dark.

'Ha ! know'st thou not that mystic man?
Well do I ken the same ;
And know the work that he performs :
The " Drowner " is his name.'

'Oh! what a fearful title 's this!
 I never yet did hear
A name that more resemblance had
 To "Executioner."

'Is then the dark foreboding right
 I had within my mind
Of his employment? Is he then
 A drowner of his kind?

'For scarcely would his fellow men
 Such name to him assign,
For drowning but the feline race,
 And, eke, the race canine.

'Perchance, some wife, to whom her spouse
 Has wish'd to give the sack,
This wretch has put into his boat,
 And never brought her back.

'Perchance, some poor unwelcome babe
 This brute, with heart of stone,
Has plunged beneath the gushing flood,
 Uncoffin'd and unknown.

'Perchance, some youthful orphan'd heir
 This cruel man of sin
Has made away with, to oblige
 The greedy next-of-kin.

'Perchance,'—'Well 'tis not quite so bad:
 Wild work your fancy makes:
His title's strange; yet does express
 The task he undertakes.

'These water-meadows' wide expanse
 Two grass-crops yearly yields,
Thanks to the "Drowner"; for 'tis *he*
 Who irrigates the fields.'

BONNET DE NUIT.

(To the Air of 'Bonny Dundee.')

'Sleep with it now.'
SHAKSPEARE.

To the waiter at Brussels 'twas Tompkins that spoke,
When he wanted a nightcap, and thought it no joke
To retire for the night, without having—d'ye see—
What, he knew not, in French was call'd *Bonnet de Nuit.*

'*Apportez-moi* something I want for *ma tête*;
For to rest I'm inclined, and the hour is quite late,'
He said, making signs to the *garçon*; but he
Couldn't *take* that Tompks wanted a *bonnet de nuit.*

The *garçon* kept smiling and shaking his head
At the signs Tompkins made, and the words that he said:
'*Je ne comprends pas*';—Oh! how wretched to be
Condemn'd to the want of a *bonnet de nuit!*

At last, in despair, Tompkins utter'd outright,
'*Apportez-moi* NIGHTCAP!'—At once from his sight
Departed the *garçon*, with '*Oui, Monsieur, oui!*'
And soon return'd bringing—no *bonnet de nuit.*

No!—A tumbler of brandy-and-water he brought,
Which, it seems, was the thing 'Nightcap' meant, as he
    thought:
And the learn'd in slang English will surely agree
That a 'nightcap' may *not* mean a *bonnet de nuit.*

There are 'nightcaps' in Oxford, and 'nightcaps' else-
    where,
Which signify 'drinks[1]';—not the nightcaps we wear:
So the *garçon* might well think a 'nightcap' to be
Eau-de-vie with *eau sucré,*—not *bonnet de nuit.*

But a French *dictionnaire* was procured, which supplied
The phrase which to Tompkins before was denied;
Who, with new-acquired knowledge elate, cried in glee,
'*Apportez-moi, garçon, un bonnet de nuit.*'

    [1] See a book entitled 'Oxford Nightcaps.'

HANGMAN STONE[1].

'Lapis sacer.'
LIVY xli. 13.
'Habet . . .
. . vetus in trivio florea serta lapis.'
TIBULLUS i. 1. 11.
'Fixus in agris
Qui regeret certis finibus arva lapis.'
TIBULLUS i. 3. 43.
'Legitima servas credita rura fide.'
OVID, *Fasti* ii. 662.

OLD stone, beside a three-cross-way, upon this verdant hill,
What would'st thou say, if thou had'st mind, and utterance,
   and will,
To tell of all the by-gone scenes, by wasting time effaced,
Which thou hast witness'd since the day which here first
   saw thee placed?

Perchance thou'dst tell of Druid forms around,—a solemn
   show,—
Co-mates of weird ambrosial oak and olive mistletoe;
Of awful rite and sacrifice,—old superstition's dower,—
And vows made to conciliate some vague-imagined power.

---

[1] A landmark between the four Devonshire parishes of Colyton,
Seaton-and-Beer, Branscombe, and Southleigh.

Or else of less mysterious rites, used at a later day,
Thou'dst tell; when o'er these fertile fields imperial Rome
    held sway;
How village swains to Terminus their festal homage paid,
And thee with garlands many-hued of fairest flowers array'd.

Perchance, thou'dst tell how here they brought the choicest
    of their corn,
And of all other various fruits that fill up Plenty's horn;
Propitiatory offerings;—the year's results begun;—
Acknowledgments of benefits;—their rural labours done.

Thou might'st relate how such things were in ages long
    before
This hill yon firs of Scottish race upon its brow upbore;
Which, from their tawny boles and limbs, a warm and
    ruddy gleam
Reflect, as though they sympathized with Phœbus' glowing
    beam:

Longer before the neighbouring grove of lofty beechen
    trees
Was grown, which, softly-whispering, sway their leafage in
    the breeze:
Old landmark of the fields! perchance, such scenes thou
    might'st declare
Here witness'd since these rural bounds were made thy
    jealous care.

Would'st thou such things relate? Thou might'st! In
    sooth we cannot tell.
One darker tale thou could'st recount, and that we know
    full well;
How once a wight, foredoom'd to death (the tale hath
    oft been told),
Shoulder'd, and to thy seat convey'd, his plunder of the fold.

Ill-fated wretch! he hither came, beneath the darken'd sky,
Conducted to this mystic place by evil destiny:
To free him from his load awhile, he thought, and take
    his rest;
And here he perish'd in his sin, impenitent, unblest.

Morn show'd that he, old stone! on thee a lifeless body
    lay,
Garroted by the cord wherewith he had secured his prey.
None knew how long his eyeballs glazed stared on the
    night-air dim,
After the agony had ceased that thrill'd each quivering limb.

Thus was he seen by passers-by,—a miserable sight,—
The victim of his own misdeed wrought on that fated night.
E'en thus, the villagers relate, he perish'd here alone,
And call thee still, thou relic quaint! in memory, 'Hang-
    man Stone.'

OXFORD:

BY E. PICKARD HALL, M.A., AND J. H. STACY,

PRINTERS TO THE UNIVERSITY.

www.ingramcontent.com/pod-product-compliance
Lightning Source LLC
Chambersburg PA
CBHW030005030726
47499CB00008B/2901